CHAPTER: PROLOGUE

One day in 2018 I struck up a conversation with a personal trainer at my gym. I mentioned that I liked to train hard even though I was somewhat restricted because of all the metalwork in my right leg. Max asked how it happened.

I showed him the bullet hole in my calf, and I told him that while helping an American client buy an old racecourse on the Black Sea I got shot by the Bulgarian mob. There was no point beating about the bush!

Over the years I have retold my story to many people. It was usually greeted with wide-eyed amazement or skeptical silence (I don't blame them; Blackpool estate agents generally don't get mixed up with the east European mafia). But Max proved to be different. By sheer coincidence he was able to give me answers to questions that had plagued me for fourteen years. I could retell *what happened* during my involvement with the mob but could never explain *why*.

Max gave me the answers I needed to make sense of the events that changed my life, events that began when an American businessman opened the door to my office.

You could say I was already in above my head...

CHAPTER 1

I was born 13 January 1966 in Bredbury, Stockport, a few miles south of Manchester. The family moved to Blackpool when I was nine. My parents split up when I was thirteen and I moved back to Bredbury with my dad and grandparents and completed my last year of high school there. After school I attended catering college in Salford.

As soon as I could I returned to Blackpool, where I got a job as a chef at the Castle Casino.

I have regarded Blackpool as my home ever since.

Later I spent a few years working in insurance when, by chance, in 1992, an estate agent customer called Martin Smith who insured his car with the firm asked me if I would like to work for him. My employer was not pleased that I was being poached by a client, but it seemed like a good opportunity for me. I agreed.

The job involved running the Belmont Estates rental agency out of Martin's office in Lytham, seven miles south along the Fylde coast. Property prices in Lytham were—and still are—significantly higher than in Blackpool, and the office seemed busy so there was potential to earn more money. Or so I thought. It also meant I spent more time away from a desk—

inspecting properties, and meeting vendors, renters, and buyers, which I enjoyed. I also helped draw up contracts, collect the rent for the clients and arrange repairs.

Generally, our clientele consisted of middle management from the two biggest local employees: BAE Systems, the arms and aerospace manufacturer, and Axa, the multinational insurance group. We didn't have to work too hard to find new clients because the office was centrally located in Clifton Square. At one stage I was responsible for 200 property rentals, which was probably more than usual but we were in no position to turn down work. The busier we became, the richer Martin Smith became—I saw none of the growth of the business because I did not get any commission, rather I was on a basic salary.

I quickly came to learn that Martin Smith's rental business was nothing without me. I did all the work. In a word, he was lazy.

Despite this, I must have enjoyed it because I ended up working there for twenty-two years. We shared a love of horse racing, and we were regular visitors to Cartmel races in Cumbria. Usually, he took me along to drive.

The property market before 2008 was buoyant, and even during the periods when the market as a whole wasn't booming, Lytham had been a desirable location for years and always attracted both young professionals and pension-rich older people looking to retire by the sea.

The first twelve years were busy, if a little uneventful. I bought a flat in a converted Catholic convent on the upmarket Winckley Square in Preston and earned enough to take regular overseas trips. I liked to travel light and had managed to squeeze in short trips to Venezuela, Panama, and Brazil (my mother's home country). These trips must have raised a red flag by security at Manchester Airport because they profiled me, which meant occasionally I would be subject to some quite insistent questioning at security. Apparently, I fitted the profile of a 30-something dodgy character who travelled the world with little luggage for short trips to exotic locations throughout the world. That certainly sounded like me.

CHAPTER 2

This settled work life would change one rainy Sunday in November 2003 when an attractive woman in her late forties walked into the office out of the rain. The working day had been deathly quiet because of the weather, so I welcomed this interlude even though I was preparing to lock up and go home.

Despite being bundled up against the rain and the wind I could see she was expensively dressed. She introduced herself as Arlene Kelly.

With a hint of an American accent, she said, 'I'm looking for a property to rent for me and my husband.'

I immediately thought, *Perhaps it was worth coming in on a Sunday after all.*

I offered her a coffee, which she gladly accepted. While sipping our drinks I showed her all our available properties to rent. She expressed some interest in a four-bedroomed detached house on a relatively new development called Cypress Point.

She said, 'This may sound like a strange request, but can I view it at five o'clock in the morning?'

Quite naturally, I asked, 'Why five a.m.?'

'I know it's inconvenient but I'm in between flights and it's the only time I have to view.'

The property was available for around £1300 per month. It was empty and I had the key— and the woman seemed serious about finding a house (and a job is a job)—so I decided to step up and show willing, even though I was not looking forward to the very early morning start.
'Sure,' I said, as if I do dawn chorus viewings all the time, 'I'll meet you at the property at

five.'

Next day I met Arlene Kelly at the house, and she seemed delighted with it.

During this time, she told me that she was a nuclear health physicist on contract to Springfields nuclear fuel production installation near Preston, a few miles away. It all seemed to check out so we did the necessary paperwork and agreed a date for her to move in, which would not be for a few weeks because she had to wait for a trailer of furniture to come from America.

Because of the high cost of rental, I also asked her for proof of income, which took some time to come. When it did arrive, it showed that she was paid by Westinghouse, the huge American nuclear fuels corporation. What also became clear much later was that she was in the UK to help negotiate the sale of the British Nuclear Fuels (BNFL) Springfields site, which went out to auction. The auction was eventually won by Toshiba for £3.1 billion. I didn't know it then, but this was information that would later become crucial for me to piece together the amazing events that would change the course of my life.

Anyway, back to the house rental. In early 2004, on the day she was due to move in, she came to the office to pick up the keys. I decided to take her to the house to make sure she had all the correct keys, and the house was ready for the new tenant. But there was a major fly in the ointment. We arrived at the house to find the locks had been changed and bailiffs had posted a letter in the window denying anyone access. The owner had not only evidently fallen behind on their mortgage payments, but they must have also neglected to pay for a new conservatory, which had been crudely ripped off the side of the building, probably by an irate builder.

Now this was my problem. Arlene Kelly had already paid-up front for the rental, and now she was effectively homeless (although she was staying at the Marriott Hotel in Preston, so she wasn't exactly on the street).

I had no other similar property on the rental books, so I had no option but to go banging on doors. We had a number of properties for sale that simply could not find a buyer. Whether the houses were over-priced (a common fault of vendors in our industry) or had bad *feng shui*, they had been on our books for far too long. I wondered if any of these owners would consider renting instead. At least they would be getting an income while they waited for a buyer.

Number 6 Plum Street was a lovely property that had been looking for a buyer for some time. The owners had already moved out, so I knew it was empty, but I took a chance and knocked on the door. By serendipitous chance the owners were there, having returned to tidy up the garden and clean the house, basically keeping it in presentable condition should the sales department arrange a viewing at short notice.

I put my proposal to them: would they consider renting to someone who was literally waiting to move in. Today. It turned out that they had recently been considering this very option. I said that I had what appeared to be the ideal tenant. They jumped at the opportunity.

I explained the major pros and cons of the new house to Arlene Kelly: the house was in a better location, being closer to Lytham, but the rent would be significantly higher: £2000 a month.

That didn't seem to put her off, so I arranged a meeting with the owners, and all went well.

She signed a three-year lease.

I wiped the sweat from my brow, having grabbed victory from the jaws of defeat.

At this moment I saw Arlene Kelly as just another happy customer who was married to a man, I hadn't yet met but would soon get to know rather too well.

CHAPTER 3

Without warning or appointment, later that winter, a man who had evidently spent his life partaking rather too enthusiastically in the joys of the great American diet—the person who would change my life forever—bounced into the office.

'Hey! Is John about?' he announced, as if talking to a large crowd.

'That's me,' I answered.

'Hey, John! Thanks for finding my wife the house on Plum Street. I'm Chip, her husband!'

There's nothing like an American to brighten up the office on a typically grey Lancashire day.

'Would you like a coffee?' I asked.

'Sure!'

We chatted for a while, as I would do with any client, during which time he told me that he possessed the rather extraordinary name of Cornelius Catlow III. Thankfully known as Chip.

Cornelius Catlow the third was in every way a European's idea of an American abroad: he was shorter than Arlene but much wider, he was loud and friendly and larger than life. And I liked him.

Once we moved on from the small talk, I asked, 'What do you do in America, Chip?'

'I sell racehorses!'

'Wow.'

'Ever heard of Travers Horse Racing Associates?'

Of course, I hadn't.

'Based in Louisville, Kentucky.'
Where else?

'I sell racehorses worldwide,' he proudly announced. 'I've had clients all over, sheiks in the

UAE, even President Putin has one of my old stallions.'

He was name-dropping to impress me. And it was working. I briefly thought, *What are you doing in Lytham if you're an international racehorse broker*? But then again, why not? His wife had a senior position at the nuclear plant, and he was along for the ride in merry old England.

Chip was a larger-than-life character—once seen never forgotten. In fact, he didn't give me a chance to forget him because he would often pop into the office on the slightest pretext— because he was out shopping or because he wanted to ask a banal question about the rental. Once he popped into the office to ask me where he could buy a car. I directed him to a dealership where he bought a lovely old Daimler and, rather curiously, a Citroën 2CV. Sometimes he popped in *just* to say hello. It was like he felt it might be impolite if he didn't pass the time of day with me whenever he was in Clifton Square. You could say he and
Arlene Kelly was the most exotic and unusual client I ever had.

One day he came into the office to tell me he had sold his company, Travers Horse Racing Associates, and that he would be spending more time in Britain. Consequently, Chip quickly crossed the line from esteemed customer to valued acquaintance. Martin Smith and I often went up to Cartmel for the point-to-point races but that year he couldn't go. On this occasion Arlene, Chip and I accepted my invitation. Another time Chip invited me to dinner at the rented property. I wouldn't say we were close friends, but he was certainly closer than most clients, who just paid the rent and you never saw them unless there was a problem at the property.

Despite his overly familiar manner - which I put down to his being American rather than any ulterior motive - I stayed friendly with Chip over the coming weeks and months. After all, he was a good client who always paid on time, hired a cleaner and a gardener to keep the rented house in tip-top condition, and was cherished by the property owners. In effect it was easy money for our business.

Out of the blue, one morning in November Chip came into the office and asked, 'Hey,

John, have you ever been to Latvia?'

Like many of Chip's questions, I would immediately ask myself, *Where is this leading*?

Little did I know.

'No, Chip, I've never been to Latvia.'

'Well, I sold a racehorse to a guy who lives there with his Latvian girlfriend. His name's

Marcus Johnson who used to be managing director of a large vegan food company.'

I put this down once again to Chip name-dropping. The story continued.

'So anyway, Marcus is looking to buy an office block over there, semi-commercial, offices at street level, residential above, that kind of thing. As you probably know, the country's due to join the EU this May and there may be money to be made in property when they adopt the euro currency.'

Anytime someone mentions property, I am interested, he quickly loses me.

'So, like I say, do you think you could go out there and see if you can help him finalise the deal and find some tenants? Generally, make sure he doesn't waste his money.'

I didn't need to say anything. He could see the skeptical look on my face.

'I appreciate how you helped Arlene find our house, so look at it as a thank you. Of course, there'll be commission for you on the deal.'

Chip gave me Marcus's number which I later called. Marcus Johnson was English and was expecting my call.

'Hi, John, Chip has told me all about you. Are you able to come over to Riga to take a look at the property? I would really appreciate a professional second opinion.'

It sounded legit, if a little unusual.

'When would be convenient?'

'How about coming out for New Year? We'll find time to take a look around the property and if you think it's okay, I'll go ahead with the deal. Then some friends of mine are having a party on New Year's Eve so we can end your stay with a little fun.'

To say it was uncommon for a Lytham property agent to visit Latvia on behalf of a client I had never met to buy a large commercial property I had never seen in a country I had never visited, would be the understatement of that particular year. These things generally didn't happen to an average Joe on the Fylde coast. I guessed that, knowing Chip's personality, there would probably be a lucrative commission in it for me and/or the agency, but beyond that no terms or contracts were ever discussed.

My reaction was one of curiosity. My thinking at the time was that I had chanced upon a client who was evidently well-connected. They say we are all presented with opportunities each day - the trick is to identify them and act on them, and, anyway, why look a gift horse in the mouth? I was in my thirties, I was single, and I was being offered a free trip to an exotic country on the Baltic Sea. There was no obvious reason to turn it down. Work generally slowed down over the holidays so it would be no hardship to take a few days off over the festive season, and my boss was keen to let me go because he would be paid a commission if the deal went through.

As Marcus and I finalised the details of my trip he suggested I bring a couple of friends along to celebrate the new year. I gave my mate Paul a call, who was keen as mustard, who also invited a friend of his called Gordon. Somehow the fact that three of us from Lytham were now going as a group allayed any misapprehensions I might have had about the undertaking.

Immediately after Christmas we flew to Riga, the capital of Latvia. Stepping out of the airport I got my first full blast of Baltic weather. It was − 10 Celsius. Marcus had arranged for us to be put up in a nice hotel on the River Daugava, which all seemed very civilised. My two mates were impressed that I had friends in high places; I acted as though the situation was nothing unusual but was still a little apprehensive about why exactly I was there.

Paul and Gordon spent the following day getting drunk and generally exploiting their good fortune, while I spent the day with Marcus Johnson. He took me to the property which turned out to be a large five-storey building spread out over a whole city block. The building looked sound and on first sight seemed a good investment for the asking price. He told me the asking price in US dollars, a figure in the hundreds of thousands as far as I can recall, which seemed very reasonable. He already had finance arranged, some of which came from his pay-off from the food company. It all seemed to be a rock-solid deal and he couldn't lose. I recommended he buy it.

It felt good to have my opinion respected by someone who was clearly operating in rarefied business and social circles I had never breached. But even at this early stage of our acquaintance, I couldn't escape the feeling that he had already made up his mind about the building. Why would he rely on the opinion of an English provincial property agent?

However, I was able to help him find a tenant. I got talking to someone in the hotel bar and happened to mention to him that a client was buying a large office block in the city. He said he was looking for an office to rent. I gave him Marcus's number and thought no more about it. Much later, after the deal was done, Marcus called me and thanked me for introducing him to his new tenant, that just happened to be Microsoft.

That more or less concluded the business side of the trip. Marcus said he was going ahead with the deal and thanked me for my (somewhat less than significant) input.

Now we were going to see in the new year with a party. But the dress code was formal, so Marcus arranged for black tie evening dress to be delivered to the hotel for all three of us. He was certainly rolling out the red carpet.

The address he gave us turned out to be a small theatre which had been given over to a private party for the night. The event was going strong when we arrived at eight o'clock. I was met with a remarkable cast of around a hundred assorted characters, who could broadly be split into three categories. The first group I noticed was a number of larger than average men - tall, wide, bulky - shadowing a number of smaller men who were weighed down by thick gold chains and bracelets, and who commanded all the attention. The third group looked like contestants from a Miss Scandinavia pageant: blonde, blue-eyed, twenties, tall, slim, enhanced.

In a nutshell, the three Lancashire lads had walked into a mafia party of gangster bosses and their trophy girlfriends being overseen by security who, when not looking out for their masters, spent far too much time lifting weights. My eyes and ears were everywhere.

Marcus was meeting my friends for the first time that evening, but he didn't seem too fussed about the fact that he was paying everybody's bill. He had reserved seats for us to watch the stage show that featured girls who came from the same stable as the trophy girlfriends, before laying on a meal. Then the party really got started.

It was difficult to pick up on the accents of the people around me because I tended to gravitate towards the people who spoke a little English, but I would say the majority were Latvian or Russian, or from the old Eastern bloc countries. I got talking to a Pole sitting next to me, a big guy who said he was a banker in Latvia. He didn't look like any Lancashire bank manager I had ever seen. He later explained that he ran his own private bank that operated from the third floor of a city centre office block. In between big gulps of aged single malt whisky, he talked evasively, never answering a question directly yet also keen to impress. He was my fantasy idea of a Baltic gangster. Except this was no fantasy. That evening he drank half a bottle of Krug and a full bottle of whisky, which didn't seem to have any effect on him. He was evidently used to sinking a bottle of scotch on an evening out. At the end of the night, he stood up—no swaying—said goodnight and walked out the door, straight as a die.

I noticed that at the head of one particular table there was a small, seemingly insignificant guy directing proceedings. Things seemed to happen around him. The small guy was probably Mister Big.

Although Marcus was the only other Brit in the room, I noticed that he seemed familiar with the tone of the party, the undercurrent of power and the illustrious guest list. It was clearly his natural environment. Perhaps he was buying the property from one of these characters.

My two friends, Paul, and Gordon seemed incurious about the circumstances of our good fortune; they were too intent on chatting up unattached pneumatic blondes and getting bladdered on expensive booze at someone else's expense. It was New Year's Eve! That's what Lancastrians do to see in the new year.

Meanwhile, my head was exploding with the amount of free Champagne on offer (Krug not Moët), the tanned flesh of the beautiful dancing girls, and the jacket bulges of the mean looking security detail. Far from my natural environment, this was another world to the lad more used to living it large on Blackpool's Promenade. And I was getting paid. Or at least I hoped so.

The three Lancashire lads staggered back to the hotel at 4 a.m. We walked across a bridge that spanned the frozen river feeling as though nothing could touch us because we had been accepted into Riga's underworld. Or at least that's what I told my drunken self.

Next morning, in my hotel room, I was woken by the haunting memory of what I had experienced the evening before. I had a good breakfast and went for a walk along the bank of the frozen river to clear my head, while the other two slowly came around with murderous hangovers.

Incidentally, to this day, Gordon—a well-travelled, hard-drinking party animal—says the trip to Riga was the best weekend he has ever experienced. Anywhere.

CHAPTER 4

On my first day back in the office, I got a typically upbeat visit from Chip.

'Hi, John, how was your trip? How was Marcus?'

I gave him a snapshot of the successful property deal and weekend of excess. 'Yea,' he said, 'Marcus said he would take good care of you.'
And how.

'Thanks for all your help on this, John. I know Marcus is grateful for what you did, and I appreciate it.'

At which point he took out a bulging brown envelope from his jacket pocket and handed it to me. I was suddenly £1000 richer.

My brain had only recently settled down to something like normal and now it was racing again. Was my advice to Marcus really worth £1000? And why was Chip paying me for the books? What was it to him, anyway?

I didn't ask.

He acted as though handing over a bung in a Lytham property office was normal procedure, and I didn't question it. I reasoned to myself that the trip to Riga was one of life's never to be repeated peculiar experiences, which would be told with gusto down the pub or at dinner parties until people are sick of hearing about it. I compartmentalised it, filed it away in a box and savoured the memory.

Looking back, I was clearly being softened up for what was to come. If I thought I was above my head in Riga, I would soon be drowning in the next dubious property deal, for which I would have to travel east.

CHAPTER 5

Later that year I took a short holiday to Singapore. I had nurtured a love of long-haul holidays for years and Singapore had long been on my bucket list. I mentioned it to Chip - he was still making his regular unannounced visits to the office - who obviously clocked the dates of my trip and the name of my hotel.

One morning on my trip I was called over by the hotel concierge who handed me two VIP tickets for that day's race meeting at the Singapore Turf Club in Changi: food, wine and a privileged view of the course included. Without a word to me, someone had arranged for me to have a day at the races. Once I thought about it, I guessed that I was being entertained, watered, and fed by Cornelius Catlow III. I felt a little guilty about his extraordinary generosity but went with the flow and had a great day out - even though I didn't have a date for the other ticket! My suspicion over my benefactor was confirmed on my return to Lytham.

Like clockwork, Chip showed up at the office on my first day back.

'Hi, John, how're ya doing?'

'Great.'

'How was your trip?'

'Good, thanks, especially my day at the races... which I'm guessing was your doing?'

'No problem, John, my pleasure,' he said, and brushed it off.

In June 2004 I flew off to Miami for a short break and stayed at the Loews Miami Beach Hotel. Like Singapore, a car came for me and took me to the Calder racecourse for a big day of racing. I was chaperoned by Bob Grim, the course marketing officer, who I presumed was an acquaintance of Chip. Bob asked if I wouldn't mind presenting the prizes to the winners, which, together with the race card, was shown live on NBC.

Later that year I was able to get a few more days off and took a flight to New York. Again, Chip took it upon himself to pull a few strings. Not only were there two tickets for me at reception, but outside was a car waiting to take me to Aqueduct Racetrack in Queens.

The car turned out to be owned by George Steinbrenner, the owner of the New York Yankees baseball team. After the races, the driver said that I had the use of the car for the evening, and he would drive me anywhere I wished. He took me to see all the sights of Manhattan at night, a trip that ended in a pre-arranged meal at Sparks Steak House, most famous for being the location of a gangland hit in 1985. I asked for the bill but was told it had already been paid.

Late in 2004 Chip opened the door to the office and came out with one of his classic non sequiturs.

'Hey, John, what do you know about Bulgaria?'

My head was probably full of rental agreements and boiler repairs, so the question flummoxed me for a minute.

'Not much, Chip… eastern Europe; ex-Communist state; CSKA Sofia is their most famous football club. That's about all I know about Bulgaria.'

There then followed a pause that I had to fill with a question, the answer to which I feared.

'Why?' I asked.

Then, as if it was the most banal conversation imaginable, he said, 'I'm thinking of buying a racecourse that's come up for sale.' I nodded apprehensively. 'Okay.'

I must admit that my mind flipped back to the Latvia deal and wondered if this proposal might also mean a foreign trip and a nice commission for me.

I said, 'I was glad to help with your Latvia deal, so if your friend needs any help in Bulgaria let me know.' 'Will do.'

The following day he came to the office clutching a briefcase that contained a set of plans.

He laid them out on my desk.

'Hey, John, this is the racecourse I mentioned.'

He obviously had the plans for a while but had waited for the right time to approach me. I had clicked open the door an inch and he had kicked it in.

'Exciting plans,' he said. 'Are you available to fly out with me to take a look at the site?

Check it over, use your expertise, evaluate the purchase, that kind of thing.'

Then he looked over to my boss who was listening from the other office. 'Can you let him out of the office for a couple of days?' called Chip. 'I want to take him to Bulgaria!'

Martin didn't seem to mind at all. My guess was that he had obviously been handsomely paid for the Latvia deal so was happy to send his colleague to Bulgaria, and wait for the commission to come in.

Chip took that as a definite yes.

'Okay, John, I'll get right on it and book some flights.'

Within a couple of days, we were both sitting on a flight from Manchester to Sofia, the capital of Bulgaria. At the time I couldn't have pointed out Bulgaria on a world map, let alone Sofia.

We were met at Sofia Airport by someone called Ivan Petrov. He handed me his business card which read: "Head of International Business Contacts Division, Republic of Bulgaria, Ministry of Agriculture and Forestry".

Chip seemed friendly with him, as if they had met before, but beyond that I don't know what their connection was. I figured that the racecourse must have been a large piece of land, so such a major purchase from a foreigner would have attracted the interest of the appropriate government department.

Ivan led us out of the airport to a brand new, chauffeur-driven, black S Class Mercedes limousine. If this was communism, it would certainly work for some people. All
Bulgarians were equal but some Bulgarians were more equal than others.

The best way to describe the muscular driver is to say he looked as though he was familiar with the same gym as the heavies in Riga on New Year's Eve. He was *big*.

Ivan said, 'We have to take another flight to Varna in a couple of hours' - another place I couldn't locate on a map; apparently, it's on the Black Sea 'so I'll take you on a short tour of the sights of Sofia.'

We stopped for a beer and something to eat. Ivan was searching for things we might have in common, which he found when he said he used to be in a band that played music from the early 1970s. He mentioned a friend of his who was in the same band.

'What does he do now?' I asked, innocently enough.

'He sells buttons.'

We returned to the airport and this time we were ushered straight through to the plane without having to check in or go through passport control. The flight took about an hour. Again, we were met by another meaty chauffeur.

We drove to Shumen, then visited a couple of hotels and various other places. Then we headed for the racecourse, which was located near the village of Balchik. The road up to the course was a narrow, overgrown country road. The car just about managed to squeeze through.

By now Chip had explained that if the deal went through his plan was to reopen the course and start a breeding operation. He also mentioned that he was interested in buying a hotel as well.

We met some people whose manner and dress suggested they were gardeners or workmen of some kind, more like country bumpkins than the kind of people who were hoping to sell a large plot of land and an ex-racecourse.

While Chip and Ivan Petrov chatted to them, I wandered around the course, which was located right on the coast. The abandoned racecourse—unused since the 1950s—was set on a huge site of 3,000 acres. We were told it had been quite something in its day, but now the original running rails were peeling and rotting, and barely showing the outline of the track. In the middle of the course there were sixty-six houses that had also been abandoned, together with a small school and a bar. The old watchtower was still standing. The local authority was making use of a portion of the unused land by growing carrots on it.

It was a magnificent site, and it struck me that the asking price of 3 million euros was incredibly cheap. Three million for

3,000 acres on the Black Sea of a country about to join the EU? It was a steal.

Chip came out to join me. He thought he would make a killing when Bulgaria joined the EU on 1 January 2007. This was much the same development thinking that went into the deal in Riga: buy up property in countries about to join the EU and wait for prices to rise as development money is pumped in. Chip's background in horse sales and stock breeding perfectly matched his interest in the course, so as far as the investment was concerned everything seemed propitious.

I was still not sure who owned the old course, possibly the municipality, which would explain why Ivan was involved in his international business role at the Ministry of Agriculture. I could find no apparent objection to the plan and said so. Not that I had any knowledge of stud farms, Bulgarian property law or racecourses (except for losing a few quid at them over the years). With that caveat, the deal had my approval. In fact, I felt a bit of a fraud. In my own mind I knew I was not offering any substantial services that they could not get from anyone locally. No one there needed anything I could offer. I was just along for the ride, as if it was a thank you for services rendered. Except that I hadn't rendered any.

Chip was pleased with my assessment, and we headed for the watchtower, where there was a besuited man waiting for us. The other guys who looked like yokels from a cider advertisement came in too, so they must have had some skin in the game.

Everyone was enthusiastic about the prospect of Chip bringing investment to the abandoned site, reopening the course, and starting his breeding operation in the country.

Ivan and the others talked in Bulgarian while Chip and I discussed the deal in more depth.

'Thanks for your approval, John, and I appreciate you coming out here. Of course, I will take care of you in the usual way.'

The deal was verbally agreed with no contracts. Nothing more than handshakes passed between them that day.

It was now getting late and, as we were preparing to return to Varna, Chip mentioned that we had not arranged a hotel for the night.

'No problem,' said Ivan, 'everything has been arranged.'

We got back in the Mercedes and drove as far as a truck stop. We stopped briefly and a man got in, who I can only describe as being the living image of a Russian gangster. He was a body double of Vladimir Putin, except bigger: shaved head, powerful, mean eyes, gold chain. Ivan said the man spoke seven languages so he could have been speaking to him in any one of them for all I knew. His name was Boris Stoyanov and handed me his business card, which read "Transcontinental Holding, Chairman of the Management Board." There were three business addresses on the card, one of which was in Riga, Latvia. That seemed more than a strange coincidence. Was he connected to Marcus Johnson and the gangsters I had met on New Year's Eve?

There were now five of us in the motor: me in the front passenger seat; bodyguard driving; Ivan, Chip and Putin/Stoyanov in the back.

We drove on, bypassing Varna, and continued on to the town of Shumen, ninety minutes inland. It was midnight by the time we pulled into the driveway of what looked like a large manor house. As we approached the darkened property, all the lights suddenly came on and uniformed staff stepped out to greet us. It was in fact a very nice hotel that belonged to the Putin look-a-like. Apparently, he owned a string of hotels and a number of businesses around Bulgaria. We were ushered into a beautiful dining room where all the chandeliers lit up just for us, where we were treated like royalty.

They fed us well even though it was extremely late by now. The night ended with an expensive cognac and cigars that were brought out of the humidor. My mind returned to the New Year's Eve party in Latvia when I was entertained with no expense spared. I just had to lap it up, be nice, don't ask too many questions, and hope that I would get paid for my time.

As the evening wound down, Boris Stoyanov turned to me, and said, 'I have nice room for you. You are here tonight. No problem.' He patted me heavily on the shoulder. 'We take care of you. In morning we have breakfast together, yes?'

The prospect of a comfortable bed reminded me of the long day we had had. The flights from Manchester, the drive out to the racecourse, the walk around the site, the strange contract negotiations over the land purchase, and the long drive back to Shumen had left me exhausted. Chip too, no doubt.

I thanked Stoyanov for his hospitality and said
that I was ready for bed. He looked at me
straight in the eye and raised a brow.
'Anything you need?'
'A couple of blondes would be nice,' I joked, and went upstairs.

My room was a stunning mix of manor house traditional and modern chic, but I was too tired to enjoy it. I was soon fast asleep. Sometime later (it's impossible to say how long) I was woken by an insistent knock at my door. In a half-sleep I opened the door to see two beautiful blonde women, hands on hips with expectant looks on their gorgeous faces. It wasn't a dream. They didn't have to say anything to make their intentions clear.

I stammered, 'Th-thanks, girls, for coming up at this hour, but, but it's late, I'm t-tired, I've got an early flight in the morning. No offence.'

They both looked as though they had lost a hand at poker, so their visit was certainly a pecuniary one. I was tempted to suggest they move along to Chip's room but decided against it.

When I shut the door, I cringed at the fact Stoyanov had taken my little joke seriously and reasoned that he must have some serious connections to be able to arrange such entertainment services so late at night. The room was hand-picked for me, probably bugged, maybe I was being filmed. To what end, I didn't know.

Next morning, I considered the events of the previous evening. Our arrival, the great food and cognac, the girls who almost became the cherries on the cake. Was I being set up for a fall or merely living a charmed life? Like my time in Riga, I tried to enjoy the largesse that was on offer, but I could never fully relax. Everything was out of my control. I never knew what was going to happen next. But until I saw something that was really questionable or criminal, perhaps I was getting myself worked up over nothing.

I had breakfast with Boris Stoyanov; neither he nor I mentioned the nighttime visit from the cheeky girls.

It was soon time to leave. He waved me off with a bottle of cognac and gave Chip a box of fine cigars. The driver took us to the airport, and we flew home.

CHAPTER 6

On my first morning back in the office it was clear that Chip had already thanked Martin in the usual way for my trip to Varna. It was nothing to him to send me abroad at Chip's bidding when he got paid so handsomely. As usual, Martin had accomplished very little while I was away, so all the outstanding work was still waiting for me on my desk.

The next time I saw him, Chip thanked me with £500+ in an envelope.

I decided to share my good fortune by booking a trip for my nephew Joe and I to go to New York for his tenth birthday at the end of the year.

As far as I was concerned, the racecourse deal in Bulgaria was done and dusted. But of course, that didn't stop Chip coming into the office every day wanting to talk about everything under the sun, including the Varna deal and how I should return to see more of Bulgaria. I was also getting weekly calls from Ivan Petrov, which always seemed unnecessary.

In April 2005, Chip came in off the street on some pretext. He brought the conversation around to Bulgaria.

'What did you think of Varna, John?'

'Great, had a fine time. I was just telling my sister and her husband about it.'

'Do you fancy going back?' he asked, seemingly randomly. But looking back, this suggestion was premeditated, and had a sense of theatre about it. 'Bring your sister,' he said, encouragingly, 'why not. Show her what it's like.'

He was very keen for me to enjoy the delights of eastern Europe once more.

'Well... I suppose I'd like to see more of Sofia. Do you know any decent hotels?'

'Sure!'

He gave me a firm recommendation.

I mentioned it again to Hazel, my sister, who jumped at the chance for a long weekend on the Continent, especially after I had told her about my experiences of lavish Bulgarian hospitality. Her husband Jeff was also on board; the only place he had visited overseas was Mallorca.
I asked Martin Smith for a few days off then booked online two basic rooms at the recommended hotel under terms that

allowed us to pay on checkout. I was off to eastern Europe once again.

We arrived at the hotel to be met in reception by a familiar face: Ivan Petrov.

'Hi, John. I had a call from Chip who said you were coming, so I thought I'd welcome you all and show you around the city.'

Another unexpected fork in the road.

We dropped the bags in our rooms, which were certainly not the standard ones I had specified online. Maybe the hotel wasn't full, and the management had given us an upgrade. As it happened, Ivan got on very well with Jeff. They were both smokers and big drinkers and seemed to have a lot in common.

Ivan took us to a café for something to eat where we *happened* to bump into his friend Emil, the glam rock fan who sold buttons, who now joined us on our tour of the city. In the course of the day Emil told us that he not only ran a business in Bulgaria but also owned a property in Washington D.C., so he must have been selling a ton of buttons.

After eating lunch, he suggested we might like to see his button operation. Selling buttons to support a property in the States? This I had to see.

I expected to be taken to a small factory, but Emil took us to his apartment, where he proudly showed us an array of coloured buttons - in his kitchen! I could see someone had been ripping off buttons from old garments and boiling them down in pots that were now filled with different coloured plastic. I was skeptical that anyone could make a living from reselling these buttons let alone enjoy a privileged lifestyle, even in Bulgaria. This seemed a strangely down market kind of business for someone who had international property interests, but it was enough to support him, his wife and his girlfriend who all lived in the same apartment.

Later Ivan took us out for another meal, this time very expensive. I guessed that the restaurant was owned by the Putin look-a-like because it had similar decor to the hotel in Shumen where I had been propositioned by two ladies of the night.

After a great night out - at Ivan's expense - he said he would walk us back to our hotel. We passed a casino, and he encouraged us to try our chances. My view was that casinos were often fronts for mobsters, and that we should steer clear, and certainly not waste our money. Still, my sister was on holiday, and she wanted a bit of fun. Ivan led her to a one armed bandit. After she fed in two coins and pulled the arm, all the lights flashed, and bells rang as the machine started spewing out coins. She had won the jackpot - the equivalent of £1000.

Ivan wore a guilty expression as the casino manager approached. As Hazel scooped up her winnings, Ivan and the manager had heated words. Now that we had emptied one of their machines, it was obvious we were no longer welcome. Clearly the machine was fixed for one of us to win. I don't know why, and I don't know how. It was just too easy.

Meanwhile, with her handbag bulging, Hazel was beginning to think that my assessment of Bulgarian hospitality was correct. We had been wined and dined since we left the airport and now, she was carrying around more money than when she arrived.

Back at the hotel, Hazel must have been whacked out from all the excitement because she went straight to bed. Jeff and I stayed up for a couple more drinks in the hotel bar. By one o'clock, after getting nicely merry, Jeff made his way to the bar to chat to an unattached girl. Meanwhile I noticed there was an entrance to a nightclub from the bar. I decided to investigate. I walked down the stairs and immediately realised that it was a strip club. The place was full of beautiful girls and one solitary punter: me, who they all wanted to make a fuss of. I was soon being spoiled rotten by this bevy of beauty - Champagne was being poured and I began to think I was in some kind of honey trap. I lapped it up, nonetheless.

Eventually I said, 'It's been fun, girls, but I'm so drunk I have to go to bed.'

Two girls simultaneously said, 'We'll come with you!'

And they did—and brought another bottle of Champagne just in case I needed refreshment. It was a great night full of double fun. No payment was offered, and despite the somewhat seedy circumstances, none was expected on their departure from my room two hours later.

Next morning, I felt rough. But I needed to get up as we were flying home that day. I forced down breakfast and braced myself to settle what would surely be a prodigious bill at reception.

I handed the receptionist my room key.

She said, 'Mr. Cheetham, there is nothing to pay.'

'Nothing?'

'Your bill has already been settled.'

Jeff? Hazel? Surely not.

'By whom?' I asked.

'Travers Horse Racing Associates.'

Chip was directing my life once more, and paying a huge bill via a company that he told me he had sold.

'What about my bill from the club downstairs?'

'Nothing to pay, sir.'

'And my sister's room?'

'All paid.'

This was more than a bit odd. Neither Hazel, Jeff nor I had put our hands in our pockets the whole weekend. Everything had been paid for. In fact, Hazel was going home a few hundred pounds to the good.

I don't think it registered too much with my sister and brother-in-law that our expenses should all be covered, they probably thought that was how international business was conducted in the property world.

However, the history of my experiences with Chip meant that I viewed this incident through different eyes. It was as if he was there at every turn. Shaping my life, looking out for me. Directing me? I could hear distant alarm bells going off but couldn't put my finger on exactly where the emergency was. Why was Chip being so overly generous? Even for a loud, brash American his behaviour was way over the top. What did he want in return? He had never asked me for anything beyond assisting Marcus Johnson with the Riga deal and accompanying him to the racecourse in Varna. But then again, I was paid for the 'work' on both occasions, so what was he (and I) doing that was so dodgy?

I had to remember that he was also a client back in Lytham and was still paying rent on the Plum Street house. My boss was taking a commission every month, so there was that to consider, and Martin never alluded to anything shifty with regards to Chip or indeed his wife Arlene, who was still employed at the nuclear power plant. Surely, she and Chip would have undergone strict security checks to even get near the place.

While it was true that some of the characters with whom I was rubbing shoulders were perhaps not exactly pillars of society, I certainly didn't see anything criminal during these trips. I have never had any run-ins with the law and would have headed for the door if I was aware of anything illegal.

I quickly dismissed my doubts about the strange relationship that had grown between me and Chip. I should say nothing, keep my employer happy, and enjoy the high life while I could.

But still I was nagged by those distant alarm bells.

Perhaps I didn't want to hear them.

CHAPTER 7

I returned to work and the daily grind.

Chip was now visiting the office daily. One day in May 2005 he said that the money was in place in Kentucky to complete the purchase of the racetrack. The document showing proof of funds had to be presented to the sellers in Bulgaria, and he asked me if I could take it to Balchik. I agreed.

I mentioned the upcoming trip at my sister's house, and Jeff asked, 'Is there room for me?'

My sister couldn't go, so why not have a boys' weekend?

My task was simply to meet somebody at the racecourse and show the document that proved Chip had the money. The letter was not sealed, and I saw that it came from a Kentucky bank in Louisville, and stated something like, "Cornelius Catlow III has sufficient funds to purchase land in Balchik for the sum of $3 million."

Jeff and I flew out in early June and stayed at the Golden Sands resort, about ten minutes outside Varna. The town was quiet and unusually cold for the time of year.

We enjoyed the first couple of days there (especially Jeff: no wife, no kids) as we waited to be contacted by Ivan. But he never arrived; his call never came.

Jeff asked if we could go and see the racetrack, so we took a taxi out to the site, about twenty-five miles away. As we approached the narrow country lane to the racecourse the taxi driver suddenly said, 'Oh, we can't drive down there!" and insisted on dropping us off in the centre of Balchik. It seemed to me that something had spooked him.

Now that we were denied access to the course, we decided to be tourists, and visited Balchik Palace, the summer residence of ex-Romanian Queen Marie (this part of Bulgaria was Romanian territory until 1940).

I noticed a few suspicious faces started to appear that day and we seemed to be followed more than once. It was never obvious enough for us to confront someone about it, but rather a realisation that we pieced together afterwards. I shrugged it off as nothing to be alarmed about.

We grabbed a taxi and returned to Golden Sands and went out for the evening.

This was a Wednesday, and we were booked to stay until Saturday, but I still hadn't heard from Ivan or Chip. Very strange. I had expected to take the document to a bank or a solicitor's office, but I was given no guidance.

I wondered if the trip was a waste of time, and I would have to re-arrange another visit.

I finally got hold of Ivan in Sofia, six hours away, and told him that I was in Varna and had brought the proof of funds. He said not to worry about meeting anyone there and that everything would be fine. He would let the appropriate people know. So, the trip was a waste of time after all.

On our last night Jeff and I went out again, but we were aware of our early flight in the morning so didn't plan on partying too hard. After having something to eat, and rather generously being invited to a stranger's wedding party, we found ourselves in the centre of Varna at about midnight. The bars were starting to close so we went to find a club that we thought may be open late. We had a few more drinks in the club and then we were ready to hail a taxi back to the hotel.

As we walked towards the exit Jeff got distracted by a girl and I went to find a taxi. The streets were empty, and I found myself walking through the old town on a walkway that spanned a small park, towards what I thought was a taxi rank.

I noticed four heavy looking bodybuilder types walking towards me. Instead of walking past they grabbed me and threw me up against the low parapet. I then saw the flash of metal and heard the unmistakable sound of a gunshot.

The next thing I remember was coming round spread-eagled on tarmac. I looked up and could see the walkway above me, about the height of a two-storey house, from where I had evidently been thrown.

My mind was trying to piece together the last few moments (seconds? minutes? I couldn't tell how long I had been unconscious), but what with my head banging, it was all a bit of a blur. The most obvious explanation for my condition was that I had fallen.

I tried to stand up but immediately fell over. I tried again. Again, I fell over. It was then

that I saw blood soaking into my right trouser leg and dripping onto the tarmac. If I had

fallen, I reasoned, I must have had a very awkward landing because my lower leg was

twisted at a perverse angle. The image returned of the four heavies coming towards me. I checked my pocket. My wallet was still there. Whatever had happened to me, I hadn't been

robbed.

I saw what I thought was the interior light of a car further down the road and again tried to walk but collapsed into a heap. I put my hands on the floor and started dragging myself backwards towards the light while trying to keep the bleeding leg off the ground. I could feel no pain. I must have been in shock with adrenaline pumping through my body.

Thank God the car ahead was a taxi. The driver, who was so close he must have seen the fall, jumped out and ran around to the rear door and helped me in. Under the interior light of the car, I could now see I had a serious injury to my leg. There was an ugly bulge under the right trouser leg that should not have been there. I pulled up the trousers and was horrified to see a huge hole in my calf and fragments of bone sticking through flesh and skin.

Despite the blood now making a terrible mess of his taxi, the cabbie said nothing. He slammed the door shut, ran to the driver's door, and jumped in.

In broken English, he asked, 'Where you stay? Hotel? Hotel?'

'No, hotel... hospital!' I spoke. 'Hospital, I'm bleeding!'

'Hotel, hotel only.'

Clearly, he had no intention of taking me to a hospital so I figured the hotel would be a safe place from which to consider my injuries and arrange for an ambulance.

I showed him my hotel room card and he put his foot down. Breaking all Varna speed records, we arrived at the Golden Sands. As if he was on some kind of timed mission, the cabbie jumped out of the taxi, ran around to the rear door, and dragged me out as far as the threshold of the hotel, leaving a streak of blood behind. Without asking for a fare, he sped off.

CHAPTER 8

The taillights of the taxi disappeared, leaving me to consider my predicament, alone and traumatised.

By now of course I was completely sober. Shockingly so. The horror of what had happened to me was now crystal clear as I became hyperaware of everything happening around me - the four men approaching, the gun shot, being pushed up against the low parapet, then the fall. And my leg! Oh, my leg.

I crawled towards the building and heaved my back up against the entrance to the hotel. My leg was a mess, I could see shattered bones, the bullet hole and torn flesh that throbbed and pulsed blood that by now was colouring my leg and foot dark purple. Hotel staff came out to see what the fuss was about but would not allow me inside. They kept saying 'Protocol, protocol' when I asked to be brought inside. They returned to reception and shut the door. I could see movement beyond the entrance, but no one came to render any assistance, medical or otherwise.

I must have been lying on the ground in this state of panic and confusion for about half an hour before an ambulance arrived. Thank God, I thought, at least someone had the sense to call for medical help. At first, I thought an ice cream van had pitched up because the vehicle looked like some kind of Communist health service relic from the 1950s.

Two guys got out of the ambulance, picked me up and manhandled me into the back. We drove fifteen minutes to Saint Anna Hospital where I was wheeled into A&E, a room that looked more like a temporary cabin. Thankfully a doctor who spoke English attended to me. He quickly assessed the damage and set to work. He pushed the shattered bones back into place and sewed up the wound. Although I was still hyperaware and taking it all in in slow motion detail, I could feel no pain whatsoever.

(Incidentally, when the stitches were eventually removed in England, I was asked if they could send them to a museum because they had used nothing like them for many years.)

I woke up hours later in a small ward with five other male patients, which I later discovered was on the sixth floor. I was still wearing my blood-stained clothing, as if I needed a reminder of last night's events—the searing pain in my leg meant I would probably never forget it. Eventually a nurse showed up with a bowl of gruel, which was supposed to be breakfast but was hardly edible. As bad as it was, at least it put something in my stomach. I was offered nothing else to eat for the next two days—and no painkillers. In fact, the staff, such as there were any, gave me a wide berth. Nobody attempted any communication, even in broken English. Nothing was explained to me about my injuries, nor was I given a prognosis, and no one seemed at all interested in the incident that led to my injury. I was in a kind of medical limbo. Meanwhile the leg had swollen to twice its normal size and the pain was excruciating.

Despite the appalling conditions in the hospital, I was beginning to worry about how I would pay for the so-called care I was receiving. Surely, they wouldn't discharge me before I settled the bill. The question of money had not yet been raised but I was sure it was coming.

And what of Jeff, my brother-in-law? Did he even know where I was? Had he returned to England on this morning's flight? Or had he been attacked by the same guys who threw me over the bridge?

I tried to think things through. Who were the guys who attacked me? If it was a mugging, why didn't they steal anything from me? If they wanted to kill me, someone was a poor shot. No, this was a deliberate warning. But a warning from whom, about what? It's possible that they were only meant to put a bullet in my leg, IRA-style, but I accidentally fell over the parapet which complicated the 'hit'. I was never meant to fall and add to the clean bullet with a very messy landing on tarmac.

On the third day six men dressed in police uniforms marched in and started roughing me up, slapping me around the face and punching me. I couldn't defend myself. I was helpless.

'What's going on?' I yelled. 'Help! Help!'

I appealed to the other patients on the ward, but they all looked away and kept silent.

One of the policemen secured a fetter to my good leg and attached it to the bed frame. I couldn't move even *without* the chain around my ankle; now I was completely immobile.

I was desperate for someone to come to my aid. I was in agonising pain, starving hungry, scared out of my wits, and now shackled to the steel frame of my bed. Anguish does not come close to describing the torment I felt.

There was a woman with the six heavies, who acted as interpreter, although their intentions were plain as day.

She thrust a form at me, and screamed, 'Sign! Sign! Mugging! You tourist, we do not care. You sign! Nothing happened.'

'I was attacked!' I yelled equally loudly. 'Thrown over a bridge. What are you doing to catch the guys who did this to me?'

'You do not see anything! Sign!'

I took a brief look at the form, which of course was written in Bulgarian, and had space for a signature at the bottom. The six guys leaned in, threatening me once more.

'Sign! Sign!' she yelled and handed me a pen.

I looked around at the other patients in the ward who were all still turned away, pretending nothing was happening. I was being treated as though I had done something wrong, yet I was clearly the victim.

What was I to do? I took the pen and signed.

My distressing night out in Varna was turning into a horror show. None of it made any sense - and makes little more sense to me as I write this eighteen years later. I imagine now how I might have cut off the leg chain then forced myself through the pain barrier and barged my way out of the hospital... how I could have hailed a taxi and gone straight to the airport. But at the time I felt helpless, alone. My resources were completely exhausted. I was also worried about the condition of my leg. I had not yet put any weight on it, and from the way it looked and felt, it needed time to heal. I imagined being unable to walk for the rest of my life or limping heavily. Could it even lead to amputation?

I didn't expect the police to return. They got what they required: a signed letter that probably stated that I had been drunk, in the wrong part of town after hours and subject to a mugging. Nothing more to see. Perhaps the higher powers were worried about bad international publicity, especially as their application to join the European Union was going through.

I fell asleep or passed out (it amounted to the same thing). I woke up in a white gown; my bloody clothes had been taken away. But rather more importantly, I was still padlocked to the bed.

I had two more days of dread, wondering how I was going to escape this hell hole of a hospital, when a friendly face appeared at the door. Jeff!

He said that since the night I left him to go looking for a taxi he had no idea what had happened to me. He had searched the streets of Sofia for me the following day and missed the flight home. By the end of the day, he was exhausted and confused and only fit to get drunk in a bar. He then hailed a taxi driven by someone who spoke a little English. Jeff shared his troubles with him and the impossibility of finding his wife's brother in Sofia. By sheer chance the cabbie said his sister was the chief of police, and promised Jeff to find out what he could about the missing Englishman. And so, he did. That's how Jeff found me in the hospital ward.

Not only was I thrilled to see him, but I was also relieved to see what he had brought: my phone, cash, and some food.

As soon as I scoffed at the food and was brought up to speed on Jeff's search for me, I called Ivan Petrov for help. I told him about being roughed up by the heavies and the form I was forced to sign, and then stressed the need to get out of Bulgaria quick. During the conversation I happened to mention that I had travel insurance (I was still worrying about the medical bill). I asked if he would call Martin Smith on the Lytham office number who would give him all the details.

We seemed to be making progress on my discharge, which was a relief to both of us. Jeff had to get home for work, and my sister must have been worried sick about us both. He didn't cope with the situation too well. He told me later that after leaving the hospital each day he would spend the evenings in a bar feeling overwhelmed and distressed by the whole situation. Which goes some way to explain why he seemed incapable of taking on the hospital staff about my appalling treatment, not to mention the roughing up I got at the hands of the local coppers.

At least now I had some contact with the outside world, which settled my mind a little and allowed me to relax. Finally, I could see the first glimpses of a route out of the hospital and a way home. That evening I fell into the first deep sleep since the night before the attack.

Ivan must have contacted Martin Smith about the travel insurance because when I woke there was a note beside my bed that indicated I had permission to fly home. Finally!

I celebrated by falling asleep once more.

When I woke up the note had disappeared. The next nurse that came into the room said, in broken English, 'We do operation. No fly. No go home. Operation!'

My heart sank. What happened to the letter giving me permission to fly home? What had changed their attitude? Should I be surprised by anything in this topsy turvy world?

When I took a minute to review the jumble of thoughts racing through my head, I realised that the letter authorising me to fly home obviously confirmed that I had medical insurance. That knowledge must have prompted the hospital to undertake an operation so as to milk the insurance. As I hadn't returned to the hotel on my last night, the management had opened the room safe where they found my insurance documents that were now in the hands of the hospital administrators. I later discovered that I had £20,000 of medical cover, exactly the amount the hospital claimed.

Two porters arrived to take me for the operation, but there was no lift, so they carried me down six flights on a stretcher. I was carried into a dirty, damp basement, which was a poor excuse for an operating theatre. I remember people around me still cleaning the rusty light fixtures as I was lifted onto what looked like a dining table that had just been wiped down.

They sat me up with my back against the wall and my legs stretched out before me. I was then given an epidural to kill the pain, which meant one thing: they did not plan on giving me a general anesthetic, probably because there was no anesthetists on hand.

I was soon losing sensation below the waist. A rather attractive nurse was brought in to hold my hand to try and take my mind off the horror show that was about to unfold. Sitting up, I had no choice but to view the entire, gory procedure, which entailed scalpels and hammers and chisels and heaven knows what surgical instruments of torture. Meanwhile the epidural was not wholly successful. The pain was agonising. Watching him saw, cut, hammer and screw metal plates and fixings into my leg was torture enough.

Once the surgeon was happy that all the pieces of bone were put back in their right places, he screwed in two steel pins to keep it all in place. Three and a half hours later they sewed me up.

After the op I expected to be taken to a recovery unit, or at least return to the ward on the sixth floor. But I was wheeled out to a busy hallway outside A&E. A few hours later another ice-cream van ambulance came for me, and I was driven out of the city. No one spoke enough English to explain what was happening. I couldn't even call Jeff because my phone had decided to die at that moment. By this time, I was not surprised by anything; I had learned to expect the unexpected.

The ambulance pulled up at a bungalow in the countryside. The house was set in its own grounds with no other properties in sight. I was stretchered in and lifted into a double bed set on wheels, the kind of which you might find in a hospital. The room was set up for one patient and had an on-suite bathroom attached. It was certainly smarter than the hospital I had just left; even the grounds were well cared for. I realised that the bungalow must have been some kind of convalescent facility, although there was hardly anyone else around except a nurse who drifted in and out of the room and one other patient in the adjoining room, but he was too far away to talk to.

Luckily my bed was up against a large window from where I could get a glimpse of the countryside. It was good to see trees and birds and the sky, and there was no chain around my leg. Then again, if the object was to keep me detained there was no need for a chain; I couldn't move for the pain in my leg, and there were no crutches to hand. I felt like I was recovering from an autopsy.

I had not arrived long before a nurse brought me something to eat - and it was edible.

While it was good to be out of the hospital, I was now virtually alone, away from the prying eyes of fellow patients. If the police returned, they could rough me up with impunity.

Now that the immediate trauma of the hospital had ended and my heart rate had returned to something close to normal, I noticed that my speech was slurred, and I had difficulty pronouncing certain words. At first, I thought it might be a consequence of the epidural or some drug they had pumped into me when I was unaware. The Bulgarian doctor had only treated the most obvious injury to my leg instead of undertaking a full examination that might be carried out after a severe fall. With hindsight I am sure I suffered secondary injuries that were never diagnosed or treated. The slurred speech has stayed with me to this day, and, on rainy days when I lift my jacket hood over my head, I get terrible neck and headache from the slightest sensation of the hood.

The next day I saw a man I didn't expect to ever see again - the last person I saw before being thrown over the parapet in Varna. Dressed in a white lab coat, as if half-heartedly impersonating a doctor, was one of the gang members who attacked me on the overpass. Now that I wasn't hurtling through the air, I had more time to assess his appearance: he was around six feet tall, well built, with dark hair.

I shuddered with dread to think that he was walking around the bungalow cum convalescent home. He gave me a subtle look of recognition, enough to put the fear of God in me, and moved on. If he wanted to finish me off, it wouldn't take too much effort.

The place was quiet and secluded and there didn't seem anyone with whom I could share my fears. There was a nursing assistant and a doctor who spoke only Bulgarian and seemed to want as little interaction with their patient as possible.

On one occasion someone came to fill a prescription, but other than that I was alone... well, alone with my minder in the white lab coat, who was at the bungalow every day, usually walking aimlessly around with some files under his arm. Was he there to keep an eye on his victim? What did he have planned for me?

One particular day was election day and what few people were there seemed to vanish. I was totally alone until an old lady came in and wheeled my bed out towards the front door and started feeding me ice cream.

It took Jeff four days to discover where I was. He brought my phone and charger, so I called Ivan (who else?) and tried to describe where I was. All I could say was that I was in a bungalow in the woods about half an hour from Varna. What could he do? Ivan was at work in Sofia, a six-hour drive away.

He never called me at the bungalow again. I haven't seen him since.

Another, more important, person who was nowhere to be seen or heard was Chip, whose dirty work I had been undertaking when all this happened to me. He did not call me once while I was in hospital or recuperating in the bungalow.

Jeff managed to come every day after that, arriving by taxi from the hotel. During all this time he seemed detached from the incredible series of events that had befallen me, well, us both actually. He must have been as bewildered by the Bulgarian health system as I was and going through his own trauma - his brother-in-law had gone missing after a night out, he had missed his flight home, then he found me in the hospital with serious injuries, before tracking me down in the convalescent bungalow in the countryside. I hoped he would have taken more control of the situation, perhaps by contacting the British embassy, finding an interpreter, speaking to the insurance company, or bringing Ivan from Sofia. But it was not to be.

Maybe he was overwhelmed by the whole affair and needed help himself. He told me he was drinking heavily at this time and spent each night in the local bars, which helped him forget everything.

Eventually I was given a pair of crutches on which I could hobble around the room. Being upright didn't diminish my sense of panic: my leg, which had not been bandaged and didn't look or feel like it was a part of me anymore, was seeping blood and pus; I was worried about Jeff not being able to return to his family and his job; I was worried about what the insurance company were doing.

My life had spiralled out of control. I was seemingly at the mercy of anyone who wanted to take advantage of me. It was a terrifying feeling to have no control over your own actions. While nothing seemed to make sense, I was simultaneously hyper-alert to everything around me, a condition that remains with me to this day, especially in situations that provoke flashbacks to that time. I believe this all contributed to my PTSD that was diagnosed by a psychologist much later on my return to England.

One thing was clear. I was alone and would have to draw on whatever resources I could muster to get through it.

After twelve days at the bungalow, I heard a car approaching. From my window I could see a woman get out of an old Lada, come into the bungalow, then click her heels all the way to my room.

She was smoking furiously as only Bulgarians can, and said, 'Come now. You go home.'

I was skeptical to say the least. I had been promised that I would go home many times in the last two weeks or so. But something about the woman's offhand manner indicated that maybe she really meant it.

She brought a wheelchair from the car and pushed it to my bedside. I hopped into the chair, and she pushed me to the Lada where she lay me out on the back seat. Notwithstanding a couple of breakdowns along the way when the engine cut out, she got me to the airport. Inside the terminal, there were no stops at security or passport control. I was wheeled straight through to the runway. They used a lift to get me up to the entrance to the cockpit of the twin-prop and pushed me through.

I remember seeing a stamp on the inside of the cockpit door "Made in Warton UK", which made me wonder if Chip had anything to do with my return home.

I made my way back to the passenger compartment to see Jeff already seated in the second row. The entire first row of five seats was left empty for the invalid. I would have expected the insurance company to arrange either a nurse to accompany me on a commercial flight or an air ambulance with a stretcher bed. To this day I don't know who paid for the flight or how it came about.

We flew to a small airfield in the south of England. I was manhandled off the aircraft and taken to a minivan—no passport control, no immigration, no customs. The van driver said he had been tasked with taking us to Preston, my home, at that time. But I had no wish to be dumped in an empty flat, so Jeff gave the driver some cash to take us both to his house in Blackpool, which he did.

For two weeks Hazel had been frantic with worry and was thrilled to have her husband home. She was horrified at the state of my leg and did her best to assure me that everything would work out now that I was back in Lancashire. (There were moments when I wondered if it would ever happen.) Hazel and Jeff's youngest child, Tommy, who was about four at the time, offered me his bed, which was more sympathy than had been shown me for weeks. It was a wonderful gesture.

I sat down and took the deepest breath of my life. Despite the severe pain I was overwhelmed with an almost physical sense of relief. And of course, the tears came. I was entitled to shed a few, considering the weeks of hell I had been through. I had made it home. The gruesome operation will live with me forever. That was my lowest moment, a time that I feared would be the end of me.

The following day I went to Blackpool Victoria Hospital A&E to get the leg checked out and have a doctor assess the handiwork of the Bulgarian surgeon.

I explained the incident in brief, then lifted the leg of my trouser, pointed, and said, 'And that's the outcome.'

They could see that I was in a lot of pain, and the stitches were seeping (there was no bandage or dressing on it by this time), so they saw me quite quickly. They took out the ancient stitches, treated the wound, took an X-ray, noticed the metalwork, and diagnosed a serious break. The A&E doctor did not feel it necessary to open up the wound to investigate further, so I was not seen by an orthopaedic specialist. They acknowledged that it was a bad break, and it would take time to heal. Be patient, they said.

The doctor did not mention the bullet in my leg, and I still did not know for sure that I had been shot.

Jumping forward by seven years, in 2012 a large package arrived at the office addressed to me. I opened it to find a series of somewhat blurred post-op X-rays that had been taken in Varna hospital. The sight of my smashed leg brought a rush of memories, which was mostly horrific. I held the X-rays up to the light and examined them carefully. I could clearly see multiple compound fractures of the tibula and fibula with embedded screws and what was clearly a thick metal rod, and a series of loose, unattached bone splinters. My knee was smashed and there were pieces of unattached bone floating. There was one small shape that did not fit the picture. It had a straight edge on one side and a rounded end.

The bullet.

CHAPTER 9

I stayed at my sister's place for a few days to recover from the whole ordeal, even though it was a small house with three children in tow, so it was tight for space.

I did my best to piece together for Hazel the previous two weeks. I appreciated the opportunity to share it with someone who showed a little empathy for my situation. My retelling of the events didn't show Jeff in a totally favourable light. I subsequently learned that the incident was a catalyst for them breaking up some time later.

My boss Martin Smith visited me after two days and seemed most concerned about when I would return to work. He couldn't accept that I had been through a traumatic, life-changing experience and needed some time to settle and gather my thoughts. Work was the last thing on my mind, but I had a mortgage to pay, so I agreed to come back into the office after three or four days. Obviously, I couldn't drive so Martin said he would pick me up in the mornings and drop me off at night, and that I could limit my duties to the office.

Since my ill-fated arrival in Varna with Jeff, there was one important person in this story who had dropped me like a stone: Cornelius Catlow III. There were no more daily visits to the office, no more invitations to the races, no more friendly *'Hi, How're ya doin'?'*

It was now many weeks since I ended up in the hell-hole hospital, wondering if I'd ever see Blackpool Promenade again. But I had not heard, seen or had a sniff of Chip. Surely, he knew what had happened to his errand boy.

Then one day a basket of fruit arrived with a short, perfunctory note from Chip and Arlene to say how sorry they were about what had happened in Varna. The basket came with a large promotional photograph of a racehorse. I believe it was a horse that Chip had sent to stud. The horse was called Protection Racket, an American thoroughbred stallion bred in Kentucky. Protection Racket... was that an unsubtle hint? I hadn't heard from them for ages so what were they playing at?

It seemed that I was no use to them anymore. They were probably more worried about the racecourse deal falling through than what had happened to their fall guy. The gangsters may have shot me, but the warning, surely, was aimed at Chip not to pursue the deal. That was basically the last I heard from Arlene and Chip.

Much later I learned that the Bulgarian mafia got the deal to buy the racetrack and turned it into a golf course.

I appreciated all the help I got from Hazel during this time, but I couldn't stay there indefinitely so it was time to return to my flat on Winckley Square in Preston.

It was a bad decision as I hadn't realised until now that my apartment block didn't have a lift, so I spent the first few days going up and down the stairs on my backside while holding my right leg aloft. Every morning Martin collected me at my front door and dropped me off at night. But this only lasted a short while; he soon roped in other people to act as taxi driver to his one-legged assistant. I managed to get in to work due to the goodwill of various people and hobbled around all day doing what duties I could.

Martin then reasoned that because I couldn't go out on appointments or conduct valuations, my salary should be cut - without any consideration or consultation with me. I resented the fact that so soon after I was lauded for taking on extraordinary tasks for a good client, my pay was cut. His true colours were shining through. I did what most people would do in these situations: I carried on. I had a mortgage to pay and had to put food on the table. With hindsight, I should have gone 'on the sick' and taken that stress out of my life, at least for a short time to allow my leg - and my tortured mind - to fully heal.

There was another source of income that dried up at this time. In my line of work there were always opportunities to buy cut-price properties from people who needed ready cash fast. I would turn these around and make a tidy profit. All that was now gone.

The leg was still far too painful to put any pressure on it and didn't seem to be getting any better, so I went to see my GP. He was not particularly stirred by my condition and told me something I was sick of hearing by now: the leg will take time to heal. Be patient.

I had plenty of time to think about the injustice of the incident in Varna. I wondered if I should report it to the British police. At work we often dealt with the local CID detectives whenever we discovered a cannabis farm at a rental, or some dodgy substance left behind by ex-tenants. I asked their advice, but they categorically said that the police would not be interested in an assault that took place in another jurisdiction. So that was the end of that.

Life continued in a similar vein for a couple of months. Martin had completely given up collecting me from home and there are only so many favours you can ask of people, so I was faced with the option of either taking a taxi or risking the train, which was a mission.

Meanwhile the hospital was calling me in for regular X-rays. They couldn't understand why the leg was not healing as it should. I'm sure I had mentioned that to them once or twice! The pain was in fact getting worse, and I noticed the leg began to discolour. Besides the pain, I became violently sick once or twice a month, which then increased to once or twice a week. Occasionally blood would be mixed with whatever I brought up.

I contacted other hospitals for second, third, fourth and fifth opinions: Hope Hospital in Manchester, Wrightington Hospital near Wigan, Oaklands Private Hospital in Salford, and the Royal Preston Hospital were all consulted. Once they looked at my X-rays (I'm sure one of the doctors actually inspected the slides upside down!), I got the same answer from each one: my leg couldn't be fixed and probably a wheelchair was the best long-term option.

Two doctors said that amputation would be preferable to a lifetime of pain. This made me angry. I got to the stage where I was questioning everything they suggested and simply refused to believe their diagnoses. Thank God I did, otherwise I wouldn't still have two legs.

Christmas was approaching, and the date of the flight to New York with my nephew. Of course, he was getting anxious that we may not be going because his uncle was still hopping on one leg. Despite the pain and distress - me being me - I decided that on balance the trip would do us both good. We flew out on Joe's birthday, a week before Christmas, which meant I spent the entire trip maneuvering my way around snowy Manhattan streets on crutches, with a 10-year-old in tow. I had to inject myself with a powerful painkiller just to get on the plane.

Eight months after my return from Varna I was beginning to lose hope of my leg ever healing. By this time Blackpool Victoria had put a cast on my leg and were changing it once a month and taking X-rays almost every week. Was this how I was going to spend the rest of my life?

I was called by a hospital administrator and asked to call in to the office for a short meeting after my next X-ray. This seemed odd. Perhaps my complaint about (lack of) treatment was finally about to be acknowledged. Before that appointment could happen, there was another intervention in my life, a most welcome one.

One good thing about working in a town centre estate agent's office is not knowing who is going to walk in the door. Thank the Lord that one day the door opened and in walked a good client of ours called Max Kirkham. We managed a number of his properties around Lytham St Annes, so he had probably popped in to drop off keys or sign some paperwork.

Max was a physics teacher at Arnold School in Blackpool.

I hadn't seen him for a while, for obvious reasons, so he asked for an update on my leg and why it wasn't healing. He probably saw how ill I looked (as well as the desperation in my eyes) together with the state of my leg which by now was turning black, and immediately decided to help.

He asked to use the office phone and dialled a number.

'Hi, Andrew, it's Max Kirkham here. I have a friend that needs some urgent attention on a bad leg break. When are you next in Blackpool?'

Max gave 'Andrew' my number and that was it - the phone call that would change the course of my treatment and the fate of my leg.

Max replaced the receiver.

'That was Andrew Clarkson,' he said, 'an old pupil of mine. He's the top orthopaedic surgeon at Blackpool Vic. He said he'll be back in town next week and will give you a ring. He's in Malawi, of all places, with his charity, Feet First.'

Max's interruption elicited bad vibes from my boss, as if he didn't like the fact that I was finally being helped. Perhaps Martin Smith and Max didn't see eye to eye. He taught Martin's daughters at Arnold.

Sure enough, Andrew Clarkson's P.A. rang me the following Monday and arranged a date for Andrew to see me.

Meanwhile I had to attend the meeting in the administrator's office. I wasn't told much other than they were aware of my visits to other hospitals, and believed a mistake had been made in my treatment and that I should have been operated on immediately I returned from Bulgaria. *Hallelujah*!

The upshot was that they gave me an envelope with a cheque inside and asked me to sign a non-disclosure agreement, so that's as much as I am allowed to say on that subject.

Even though the cheque was made out in my name, I signed it over to the charity's bank account. I should have taken a photograph of the cheque and stuck it on my wall as proof that I wasn't talking nonsense during those visits to hospitals throughout the northwest.

In good time I received a date in March 2006 for the operation, due to take place at a small satellite hospital in South Shore. Obviously, it meant taking time off work, but all Martin wanted to know was how long I would be away from the office. I told him it would take as long as it took. The operation was scheduled for a Friday, which would be the last full day of care at the site because the hospital was being decommissioned that weekend. Someone must have been smiling down at me.

The operation was a mammoth four hours long, but this time I was not propped up on a dining table inspecting the gruesome insides of my damaged leg. However, I was awake, but this time I was enclosed in a surgical bubble and couldn't see Andrew working on my leg. Also, they gave me powerful painkillers! I was being spoilt.

The surgeon kept me informed throughout the operation, which included telling me that the Bulgarian metalwork was rusty and that I was very fortunate to be alive. During the op they took some bone from my hip to replace some of the smashed bone in my leg.

It took thirty-six pieces of metalwork to straighten my leg—plates, pins, and screws. He showed me the heavy metal rod from the first op that he had replaced, but he wouldn't give it to me as a trophy. The reason my leg was turning black was that the Bulgarian doctor had used two different metals that had reacted against each other and began to corrode.

After the op, Andrew clearly wanted to manage my expectations when he said that I would have great difficulty walking as I did before the incident, but he didn't think it impossible that I could at some point lose the crutches. Although I may not walk as I once did, I had to believe that Andrew and his team had saved my leg. I also believe he took out the bullet fragment when he removed all the Bulgarian metalwork.

Following a very welcome hospital visit from Max Kirkham (the only person who made the effort), I was discharged the next day and taken home by ambulance. The driver couldn't believe that I lived on the first floor with no lift, and watched agog as his patient climbed the stairs in reverse on my backside.

That same day my boss called round at my apartment to ask when I was likely to be back at work. I remained vague and said I didn't know.

Without further discussion, he said, 'I'll pick you up on Monday.'

I survived the rest of the weekend at home alone.

Monday morning came too soon, and sure enough Martin was on the doorstep pressing the intercom downstairs, waiting to drive me to work.

But it was far too soon to get up from my sick bed. On arrival at work, I was violently sick and brought up a worrying amount of blood. Martin called an ambulance, and I was taken back to hospital. They diagnosed blood poisoning. Nine months of rusty metal in my body had to have an effect on my bloodstream. The treatment took a few days during which time I made sure no one touched my leg.

CHAPTER 10

Once I felt more like myself, I returned to work. During all this time I was struggling to pay my mortgage because Martin had pared down my income. I felt as though I was forcing myself to attend work. I suppose I could have resigned and struggled on benefits, but I had little choice. It was either work or starve. I was determined to think positive thoughts and hope for a brighter future. As much as I complained about my boss, work was a blessing at this time because it gave me a reason to get out of the house. It kept me sane. Sort of.

One day at work I received a call from a friend of a friend who was a personal trainer called

Andy Ashton. I explained what had happened to me and he suggested attending the Virgin

Gym in Preston, where he worked. This sounded like a strange suggestion as I had been

told that it was unlikely, I would walk again unaided.

Something told me to believe in Andy. That night I walked on crutches two miles downhill to the gym. It might seem an extreme way to get a little exercise, considering my condition, but it gave me a goal to reach. I spent a short while with Andy then somehow managed the uphill journey home. I kept at it and did this for months, although I didn't notice making any progress. Or so I thought.

Then Andy told me he was travelling to the USA to enter a fitness competition and would be away for a few weeks. In fact, he went on to win Fitness Champion of America and became the face of Abercrombie and Fitch.

Meanwhile his client in Preston was not doing so well. I stopped going to the gym during this period but found another form of exercise. Every night after work I would walk down the long entrance slope into Avenham Park and then battled my way home on one leg.

My financial health was no better than my physical health. I had not been able to keep up with the mortgage payments on my flat, so it was inevitable that the bank would call time on the loan. I got the dreaded red letter that told me my home was due to be repossessed. I decided to fight with whatever I had to keep the flat, so I attended court on crutches and explained my situation. The judge was astounded by my story and gave me a suspended order, a period of time within which I must try to pay the arrears. I was thankful for the reprieve.

Days turned into weeks, then months and the cold weather came around again. Feeling a bit more mobile, I decided to go Christmas shopping on crutches. My efforts struggling up

Winckley Square into Preston looked more like something from a comedy sketch. I went into Marks & Spencer and took the escalator up to the first floor. Well, getting on was okay but, as I soon discovered, stepping off a moving stairway on one leg is nigh on impossible.

As I approached the second floor, I went into panic mode and collapsed on the moving escalator. Somebody pressed the emergency button and the staff ran to drag me off and seat me on a chair. Then I was rather gracelessly pushed along on the chair with no wheels into the staff lift so I could return to the ground floor.

I came out of Marks & Spencer absolutely destroyed. I wondered how on earth I was going to get home, but I battled on and somehow made it. I spent that night crying myself to sleep while contemplating ending it all. It really was becoming too much. I faced a huge battle to get back onto two feet, but I felt so alone, I had no one to lean on (no pun intended).

Next day was Sunday so I spent the day in bed—I felt as though there was nothing worth getting out of bed for. I didn't eat a thing; I just lay there wishing the day would end.

Once again Monday came too soon and I was dragged off to work. That afternoon Martin sent me to make a cash deposit at the bank, which was only fifty yards from the office. I was grateful to get out even though it was chilly. It had been a very cold night and frost was still on the ground. The inevitable happened. I slipped and severely hurt my bad leg. At home that night my bruised leg turned black and blue. This set me back months, in confidence as much as physical healing.

How was my nightmare going to end? The daily grind of work coupled with the precarious situation with my mortgage and the consequent fear of receiving a red letter from the bank felt like I was living in a real-life version of the movie *Groundhog Day*.

With one notable interruption.

Earlier I mentioned that I hadn't seen Ivan since he treated Hazel, Jeff, and me on that short break in Varna. But I did *hear* from him. Curiously, he called me at home on New Year's Eve.

The call went something like this: 'Hi, John, it's Ivan!'

Imagine a prolonged silence here. I was too dumbfounded to speak.

'How are you?' he asked. 'Just checking that everything is good with you.'

I didn't know how to respond. When I gathered my thoughts, I answered, 'I'm fine, how are you?'

There was no other small talk and nothing more profound than that. He called me on the following New Year's Eve, and the next, and every New Year to the present day.

I find this very odd behaviour, considering the history of our association. Guilt? I don't know for sure, but I think he knows more about the Varna affair than he is letting on. Perhaps he was pre-warned that something could happen to me from forces that were working to prevent the racecourse deal from going through. A dispassionate observer may think the attack was not only a warning to me but to everyone who was involved in the land deal. But I was the only one who suffered the consequences.

My birthday came round and the girls at work bought me a cake and played Elton John's

"I'm Still Standing". This is still my tune to this day...

The small celebration gave me a lift and encouraged me to continue my walks in the park on fine days. Every day I tried to weight-bear a little more on my bad leg. Every day I would collapse in a heap. It didn't deter me.

My speech was still slurred so I had to relearn how to speak as well as walk. Perhaps I got a head injury in the fall. I was certainly concussed because there was a period of time after being thrown over the bridge parapet that I cannot recall.

I couldn't keep the wolf (i.e., the bank) from the door forever and eventually my home was repossessed. Even though I knew it was inevitable, it hit me hard. Someone who had made his living from property for years had been thrown out of his home. It was another nadir in an increasingly frequent series of low points in my life, and a blow to my sense of self-worth and any ambitions I might have had for a comfortable future.

I shared my woes with the Turkish owner of a kebab shop around the corner from the

office.

Ahmet put his hand in his pocket and handed me a key. 'Here you go, John. Here's the key to the flat upstairs. Stay as long as you want.' I asked him how much I owed him. 'Nothing,' he said.

I was overwhelmed. Rescued by a kebab shop.

This was a lifesaver. Despite my mortgage difficulties I had to look on the bright side: I had a roof over my head and the new location meant I could hop to the office in two minutes. I stayed in Ahmet's flat for nine months.

The bank took possession of my apartment in Preston and eventually sold it at a huge loss.

During all this time I never heard from Arlene or Chip. I was evidently no use to them anymore. Then one day a random postcard from them arrived at the office from South Africa, explaining that Arlene had been posted to Johannesburg. It couldn't have been less personal. I found it astonishing that they would act as though nothing had happened over the last few years.

I continued my efforts to get mobile. My new neighbourhood meant I could hop up and down Lytham Prom or around the local park, Lowther Gardens. Surely by now there should have been a notable improvement in the condition of my leg. It hadn't touched the ground in a year. I was not offered physiotherapy and just had the occasional call from Blackpool Victoria asking me to attend another damned X-ray. I stopped going. This was the period in which I paid for private consultations with a stream of know-all doctors.

The year was turning, and I still couldn't walk without my crutches. Depression was getting to me. Inevitably I fell at home which set me back yet again. I returned to the hospital for yet more changes of plaster cast and shoe fittings. My leg was getting so thin and weak it looked like something a chicken would be proud of.

My life had shrunk to hopping to work, hopping to the shop, then hopping home. I needed a mental escape, so I was reading voraciously at this time and avidly watching travel shows on TV, which represented a kind of dreamland of possibility. I was living vicariously through the adventures of various travel presenters, in particular Varun Sharma's show: *Inside Luxury Travel*. I wrote to him. We are still friends today and I was delighted when we were able to meet.

In time I found that I could bear to gently place my bad leg on the ground on occasions, although I was usually in pain or quickly lost my balance. It was a 'step' in the right direction.

Martin and I were still going to all the Cartmel race days. That year (he drove for a change) I had to watch the races standing on one leg looking like some kind of deformed flamingo holding onto the perimeter rail.

Martin and I had been going to the races for twenty years and usually bought an annual pass that allowed us entrance to all seven or eight race days throughout the year. Around this time an official from the racecourse wrote to me and said that they had heard about my difficulties that occurred while trying to buy a Bulgarian racecourse for a client, and would I mind if they named a race after me. I was thrilled.

This didn't happen for some time as I thought it would be good to be able to walk before my race day at Cartmel. It gave me something to aim for and pushed myself even harder to get fit. I carried on trying to work, trying to walk, breaking down in tears daily and pushing myself beyond what I thought were my physical and emotional limits. Thoughts of suicide crossed my mind more than once.

Despite my down days - and some of them were very deep - there was no doubt that weight-bearing seemed to be easier on certain days, so, yes, I was improving. My trips to the gym had helped after all. What became apparent at this time was that the smashed leg was an inch shorter than it used to be, but I could easily compensate for it in my gait, so it was not too noticeable.

Cartmel race day came about: 16 July 2009, to be precise. They called it the John Cheetham Handicap Hurdle, due to run at 4.50 p.m. Despite my best efforts to be fit for the race, I still couldn't walk unaided. The racecourse allowed Martin to park his car on the rail so I could at least watch the race in some comfort in the uncommonly brilliant Lake District sunshine. For posterity, allow me to announce the result:

1st   More Equity

2nd Mystified

3rd Rare Coincidence

I was asked to come up to meet the winner, so out came the crutches and I hopped to the podium. It was something special to present prizes at a race in my name, and the whole experience gave me another great boost.

Since my op at Blackpool, I had continued to be sick two or three times a week with no apparent cause. I reasoned that the rust was still in my body and had become embedded in my central nervous system. I never felt truly well.

The doctors didn't know how to treat it, as usual.

But - slowly, slowly - I was taking short walks without help. The leg could finally take my body's weight. Later that year the crutches were finally disposed of, and I began walking unaided, albeit at a snail's pace. This only made Martin push me at work even harder. He quite liked controlling me.

In 2014, when I was able to walk more freely, if a little unsteadily, my sister booked me a holiday in the resort of S'illot on the east coast of Mallorca. But she had an ulterior motive.

I would soon find out what that was.

This was the first time I had been through airport security since my op, with inevitable consequences. The metal plates and thirty-six pins in my leg set off every alarm they had. Ever since, I have kept pictures of the X-ray on my phone to show security. (Warning to other travellers: don't get behind me at airport security; it might take you a while to get through.)

I began travelling solo once more in 2009 and I had a terrible time getting through security in Japan and was refused point blank to get into Tiananmen Square in Beijing. It might seem like I travel a lot for a property agent but it's important to me; sometimes I think it's the only thing that keeps me going. I should have been a travel agent instead of an estate agent!

Unfortunately, my first trip to Mallorca coincided with the first snowfall on the island for twenty years. Despite gingerly making my way around the icy ground, I enjoyed the trip, especially the capital, Palma.

On my return, Martin picked me up from Manchester Airport and immediately took me on two appointments to value houses. Why couldn't he have done them while I was away?

Seemingly out of the blue - but actually something my sister had been brewing for some time - Hazel asked if I would move out to Mallorca and run a bar for her. She had bought it together with a small flat in S'illot from her redundancy pay-out at Guardian Royal Exchange. So, my last visit wasn't quite as innocent as it appeared.

Work had been getting me down lately and she probably got me at another low point. Without thinking too much about it, I said, 'I'll go!'

Of course, I told no one.

She promised me a salary and free accommodation, so it sounded ideal. It wasn't.

Some weeks later, I spent my last Sunday afternoon collecting rent for Martin. Even though I was owed outstanding back-pay, on the Monday morning I placed the collected rent money and my office keys on my desk and wrote Martin a note: 'Bye!'

Which was all he deserved.

Later that day I was on a plane to Mallorca for a new life.

Hazel had bought the bar as a going concern, except it wasn't going anywhere. The bar had evidently been closed for some time, so I did my best to clean it up and get it ready for paying customers. The bar was located in a part of town that was awash with all-inclusive resorts, so there was little need for a bar aimed at passing trade. I knew the little venture would fail from day one.

On day two the apartment was robbed while I was at the bar waiting for my first customer.

The thieves took everything I owned.

My new life was certainly starting on the back foot. The bar was deathly quiet, and my sister justified not paying me because the takings were so low. The bar took 10 euros on a good day, so that was all I had to live on. The weather was warmer than the UK but with no money in my pocket it hardly mattered where I was.

After a dreadful year I received a call from an estate agent in Blackpool town centre. They knew me and my experience so offered me the office manager's job that was due to start on 2 January 2014. I had squeezed everything I could out of my year in the sun, and I was as relaxed and tanned as I had ever been. Penniless, but relaxed. But it was time to go back to my roots.

Hazel sent me plane tickets to return home for Christmas, thinking I was returning to

Mallorca in the new year. Of course, that didn't happen, and I started work at Metcalf's on

Topping Street. My new employer knew nothing about my lingering injuries and sickness

so, I decided to keep the gory details from him.

As I had returned with virtually no belongings, I had to move quickly to get ready for my first day back at work. Metcalf's had an empty flat on their books that they couldn't rent, so I took it on. I needed a bed, so a supplier that I had used countless times through Belmont Estates came to my rescue. A men's outfitter gave me a suit. It was good to know that I had made some valuable connections in my years as a property manager.

Shortly after moving into my empty apartment in Blackpool, one Saturday morning a white van pulled up outside. The driver said he had a delivery for John Cheetham. This was strange because nobody knew I had moved except the owner of the property and my new boss. The driver gave me a padded white envelope, which I could tell contained a bottle. I asked him where he was from, and he said that he had been sent by British Nuclear Fuels to deliver the bottle. Very odd. The only person I knew with that connection was Arlene, who I hadn't heard from in nine years. I opened the package to find a bottle of liquid similar in consistency to cough syrup. The bottle had a label that said, "Provided to the people of Chernobyl". I Googled it and discovered that some people used the drink as a kind of detox.

Of course, I didn't drink it, or indeed touch the bottle again. Joker or concerned individual?

I never discovered who sent it.

I left Metcalf's after nine months. The partners of the business split up, so my position became untenable. Still, I was grateful for the original offer of the job which enabled me to return to England.

I then took a job as general manager of a holiday park in Morecambe, an offer that came from a connection I had made at Belmont Estates. It seemed a good fit for me even though it was a ninety-minute commute. The job was very much like property managing and estate agency: overseeing sales, collecting rent and fees. Instead of houses it was caravans.

I liked the job so much that after a few months I decided to move up to Morecambe instead of travelling back and forth every day. Also, I had decided that if finances allowed, I would try to buy another property. The regular income meant that banks once again viewed me as a good risk to take on a mortgage, but the offer of a loan came with a caveat. My old mortgage company (the one who foreclosed on me) would put a line on the new property until the outstanding debt was paid off. I am still paying off the mortgage shortfall today.

CHAPTER 11

Ten years after my misadventures in international property and brush with the eastern European mafia, I found myself settled in a new life in a new town. My leg had largely healed, my limp was hardly noticeable and the details of the trips to Riga and Varna were becoming a blurred memory. Sometimes it was like looking back on someone else's life— until I caught a glimpse of the gruesome scars on my leg.

Intent on getting as fit as I could, I joined a gym in Morecambe. One day I struck up a conversation with a personal trainer, Max. He had a faint American accent which he had picked up while working for his father who ran a fibre optic company in New York. I mentioned that I liked to train hard at the gym even though I was somewhat restricted because of all the metalwork in my right leg. He asked how it happened.

I told him that while helping an American client buy an old racecourse in Bulgaria I got shot by the mob. When Max lowered his eyebrows and closed his open jaw, he mentioned that his father had racehorses in New York. I mentioned Chip's full name: Cornelius Catlow III. Let's be honest, once heard never forgotten. He gave me a look of recognition, as if cogs were twirling in his mind.

The following day we met again at the gym. The first thing he said to me was that he had spoken to his father about my story, who had put two and two together and came up with a theory about what happened to me. Coincidentally Max's father had bought his racehorses from Chip, and he knew more about his background than I did. He believed it wasn't a racecourse I was sent to buy in Bulgaria. His father was sure that I was used as a front to buy the 3,000-acre course in Balchuk as a site for a future nuclear power station. His theory was that Chip's interest in buying the racecourse was hiding the fact that he was buying the land for his wife Arlene (who he already knew was a nuclear physicist), who was in turn acting for her bosses at Westinghouse, the nuclear fuels giant. The mafia clearly had interests - perhaps coal or gas - in opposition to nuclear power.

This theory came as a shock to me, and yet it all made sense. The pieces now fitted together. I was shot by the Bulgarian mafia to scare off Chip, who was fronting for Arlene who was acting for Westinghouse. To distance themselves from the dirty business, everyone involved in the racecourse deal needed a patsy, a fall guy. And they found one: me.

And yet I have no proof whatsoever. But I don't need any evidence to believe it. Unaware of my part in the transaction, I got caught up in a complicated web of greed and power.

There are many questions still unanswered - and perhaps never will be.

Had I been softened up from the day Chip first opened the door to my office?

Was the first deal in Riga a test to see if I would comply with their directions?

Was Chip involved with the mob?

Did he know more than he was letting on?

Did Ivan Petrov know the mob were involved in the incident on the Varna bridge? (But then again, he seemed to be the only one person with a conscience. Without him I would be dead.)

Was the photograph of the horse called Protection Racket a joke or a sinister warning?

Was Martin Smith involved in the foreign deals beyond receiving a simple commission?

One question I could answer was that as soon as the mob sent their heavies for me on the Varna bridge, no one had any use for me anymore. One minute I was the centre of attention and worthy of lavish hospitality, the next I felt like a pariah.

From that moment my life changed inexorably. I have been mentally scarred from my experiences, but I deserve to tell my story. The principal joy in my life that keeps me going is long-haul international travel (with the exception of Bulgaria, of course). I don't feel as though I'm going on holiday unless I'm on a ten-hour flight. It's so important to me that sometimes I feel as though I would rather miss a mortgage payment than miss a holiday.

Some days I believe I have been fortunate... saving my leg from amputation... bumping into Max at the gym... surviving. I have always been a glass-half-full kind of guy. I'm a survivor and live everyday as though it's my last and learn everyday as though it's my first.

But - and there is no point denying it - the trauma remains, and occasionally bursts out in unexpected situations. For instance, in 2022 I took on a job as manager of an estate agency in St Annes that had a kitchen and toilet in the basement. I found it difficult to cope with the claustrophobia in the kitchen which provoked a visceral reminder of the nightmare operation in Varna hospital. I would go downstairs for a cup of tea and end up in tears, frightened someone would pick me up and place me on an operating table. After one particularly bad episode in the agency kitchen I returned to the office and told them that I simply couldn't cope and went home. I never returned. I had only ten weeks in the job. They said they understood my predicament, so paid me off and nothing more was said.

In other public spaces, such as restaurants, I have to sit with my back against a wall so I can see the exit. This behaviour will be familiar to any fellow sufferers of PTSD.

I suffer occasional bouts of sickness, but I can contain it if I avoid certain foods. I am also subject to shooting pain in my leg. Consequently, my GP has referred me to Eye Movement Desensitization and Reprocessing (EMDR) to try to overcome some of the torment.

Finally, I have to deal with the fallout from the Varna incident in my own mind, and for that I have to draw on my own resources. Writing *The Fall Guy* has helped. Following a degree of success with my poetry, an album of songs and writing this book, I have been encouraged to continue writing. My plan is to return to university and take a degree in English and creative writing with the aim of teaching English abroad, preferably somewhere warm. But will always keep a base in Blackpool, my adopted home.

"I now live everyday as though it's my last and learn everyday as though it's my first".

"Although, I have been told that I'm a danger to society and, to myself maybe, I'm just being protective and resourceful. Maybe, it's the aftermath of surviving a mob hit?"

John Cheetham

Testimonials

Thanks John, you are a superstar as far as Fylde Coast Radio is concerned.

Printed in Great Britain
by Amazon